For information address Disney • Lucasfilm Press,
1101 Flower Street, Glendale, California 91201.

Printed in China
First Hardcover Edition, July 2016   10 9 8 7 6 5 4 3 2

ISBN 978-1-4847-8670-3
FAC-023680-17198

Visit the official *Star Wars* website at: www.starwars.com
This book was printed on paper created from a sustainable source.

STAR WARS

The Battle of Endor

DISNEY | LUCASFILM
PRESS

Los Angeles • New York

Book Twelve

Han Solo and Princess Leia carefully peeked over the forest foliage.

"The main entrance to the control bunker is on the far side of that landing platform," Leia said. "This isn't going to be easy."

Han and Leia were on the forest moon of Endor on a mission to take down the shield protecting the Empire's Death Star. If Han and Leia didn't succeed, there would be no way for the rebel fleet to destroy the weapon. Unfortunately, the way to the bunker was blocked by a platoon of stormtroopers and Imperial officers.

Behind them, Wicket the Ewok began to talk to his friend Paploo. The two Ewoks seemed very excited.

"What's he saying?" Leia asked C-3PO.

C-3PO explained that the Ewoks knew about a secret entrance to the bunker.

The rebels followed Wicket around the Imperial base to a second doorway. There were fewer biker scouts at that entrance.

"This shouldn't be too much trouble," Han said.

But before Han could do anything, Paploo ran out of hiding and grabbed a speeder bike. Then he raced into the forest on it!

The biker scouts rushed after the Ewok. It was the diversion Han and Leia needed!

While C-3PO and R2-D2 waited in the forest, the rest of the rebel troops hurried into the bunker. Han and Chewbacca quickly got to work planting charges.

But before Han and Chewbacca could destroy the shield, a new platoon of Imperial troops rushed into the bunker. Chewbacca growled, but there was nothing he or Han could do. They were caught!

Meanwhile, above Endor, Lando Calrissian flew the *Millennium Falcon* toward the Death Star. The rest of the rebel fleet flew behind him, readying their attack.

Lando looked at the ship's controls. The Death Star was jamming their readings. Suddenly, Lando realized that the Emperor must have discovered their plans. The Empire knew they were coming!

Out of nowhere, Imperial TIE fighters raced toward the rebel fleet, firing away. The rebels had to defend themselves until their friends on Endor could destroy the shield.

Back on Endor, C-3PO and R2-D2 had a plan.

"Hello! I say, over there! Were you looking for me?" C-3PO cried out to the Imperial troops from his hiding place in the forest.

Stormtroopers ran to capture C-3PO and R2-D2, but just as they reached the droids, there was a great battle cry. It was the Ewoks!

Han and Leia watched in amazement as the Ewoks attacked. They shot arrows and slung rocks to take down the stormtroopers. Some Ewoks even attacked the Imperial forces from the air!

With the Imperial forces distracted, Han and Leia had no trouble escaping. It was time to get back to the bunker and take down the shield!

But when Han and Leia reached the bunker's doors, they were closed tight. This was a job for R2-D2.

"Artoo, where are you? We need you at the bunker right away," Leia called over the com-link.

Across the battlefield, R2-D2 whistled at C-3PO. The two droids raced over to the bunker to help their friends.

Meanwhile, Lando saw the Death Star fire on the rebel fleet. He was surprised. The Death Star wasn't supposed to be operational yet!

Admiral Ackbar, the leader of the rebel fleet, saw it, too. "All craft prepare to retreat," he said.

"Han will have that shield down. We've got to give him more time," Lando replied. If the rebel fleet retreated now, they wouldn't get another chance to destroy the Death Star.

The Ewoks were still bravely fighting the stormtroopers. With a great crash, the little creatures released an avalanche of logs to bring down an Imperial walker! But soon another walker took its place. Han and Leia needed to get into the bunker—fast.

R2-D2 reached Leia and Han. He had just plugged into the bunker when there was a great explosion. The droid was slammed against the bunker door and sparks flew everywhere. R2 was hit!

Han looked at the droid in alarm. "Well, I suppose I could hot-wire this thing," he said, getting to work on the panel.

But before Han could open the door, an AT-AT walker stomped up and stopped right in front of them!

Strangely, the walker didn't fire. Instead, the top hatch opened. It was Chewie! He and two Ewoks had stolen the machine. That gave Han an idea.

Han used the AT-AT's communications to trick the Imperial officers into thinking the Rebellion had lost the battle. When the Imperials opened the bunker doors, they were met by the rebel army!

With the Imperial forces defeated, Han and Chewie quickly finished planting the charges. Moving his troops away from the entrance, Han blew up the bunker. There was a huge explosion! The bunker was destroyed, taking down the Death Star's shield.

Now the rebel fleet could attack the Death Star's reactor. Lando flew the *Millennium Falcon* through a gap in the Imperial defenses and into the long corridors of the Death Star. But the rebel forces weren't alone. TIE fighters flew in after them, firing laser bolts!

One rebel pilot, Wedge Antilles, spotted the main reactor. Wedge and Lando both fired. The reactor exploded into a million pieces.

Together, they raced back toward open space, but the corridors were collapsing around them. There was a fiery explosion from the destroyed reactor—and it was gaining on them! Lando and Wedge didn't have much time.

The rebel ships reached the end of the tunnel just in time. They shot into space as the Death Star exploded behind them!

That night, the rebel troops celebrated with the Ewoks. Lando, Chewbacca, and Han hugged—friends until the end. C-3PO danced with Wicket as R2-D2 whistled in celebration. Soon Luke joined them. Leia ran to hug her brother, the Jedi Knight, who had survived his battle with the evil Emperor.

Luke smiled, glad to see how happy his friends were. As he stepped away, he saw the Force spirits of Jedi Masters Obi-Wan Kenobi and Yoda. And there with them was his father, Anakin Skywalker, once again a Jedi. Luke hoped he could make them proud.

Leia ran over to pull Luke back to the celebration. They had so much
to tell each other. But it could wait. Tomorrow, the galaxy would awaken
to a new day without the Empire: a day of freedom, possibility, and new